Melted Promises
A Poetry Collection

Farzana Habib

Ukiyoto Publishing

All global publishing rights are held by

Ukiyoto Publishing

Published in 2024

Content Copyright © Farzana Habib
ISBN 9789367958339

All rights reserved.
No part of this publication may be reproduced,
transmitted, or stored in a retrieval system, in any form
by any means, electronic, mechanical, photocopying,
recording or otherwise, without the prior permission of
the publisher.

The moral rights of the authors have been asserted.

This book is sold subject to the condition that it shall not by
way of trade or otherwise, be lent, resold, hired out or
otherwise circulated, without the publisher's prior
consent, in any form of binding or cover other than that in
which it is published.

www.ukiyoto.com

DEDICATION

This book of poems is dedicated to Rishabh Matya
Thank you for the memories, experiences, and lessons.
I am grateful for your presence and will always remember
you

Contents

Time	1
Signs	2
New Feelings	3
Crack	4
Your Scent	7
A Win	8
Like a Fool	9
The Next Meet	11
Words From the Heart	13
Livin'	15
Sinner	16
Opening Up	17
Challenge	18
Dawn's Eyes	19
Overdoing It	20
The Gift of Love	21
Dreams	23
Home	25

Double Ended Sword	27
Fading	28
Final Message	30
About the Author	*31*

Time

Each day has the same 24 hours
But every second, minute and hour drag on
I did not know what was happening at first
But soon realized it is all because of you

Signs

Smiles appear out of nowhere
Silence turns into laughter
Single messages to texts
Texts to calls
Calls to meets
Meets to plans
Plans to memories

New Feelings

I have felt lonely before
This time it feels different
It ends with an ache

I have been impatient before
This time it feels different
It is plain irrational

I have been angry before
This time it feels different
It melts away quickly

I have been sad before
This time it feels different
Tears gather

Crack

It came out of nowhere

I was finally beginning to feel comfortable

Thought I could stay here a bit longer

I might have been on a high the last couple of days

A glorious high

The words you uttered over the phone the other night

Brought me down

Fast and hard

I was wondering if I am wasting time with you

The worst thing you could have possibly said to me

What was I wasting then

Time

Feelings

Effort

Everything felt natural

At least from my end

Calm like the ocean

Warm like a crackling fire
Things must have changed
When had that happened
I did not even notice
Are you getting ready to leave then
You led me to hope for something more
What was all that for
All the times you said you liked me
Or something about me
The way your eyes held on to mine
Drew me in
The way you held me close
Traced every line and curve
The way our bodies melted
I cannot think about any of it now
Was the love I felt the truth
Or another glittery lie
In no condition to debate
I do not really want to hear myself think
Red liquid fills up one glass after the other

Is it being poured by someone else
Or am I doing all the pouring
I cannot be sure of it right this minute
Maybe it will numb my senses
At least for the remainder of the night
The music continues to play
But it sounds so far away

Your Scent

I still have your scent on me

The deep smoky fragrance follows me everywhere

I can still feel your fingers traveling through my dark tresses

I can still feel your lips on mine

Like they were made for only me and no one else

I can still feel the silken touch of your hands on my skin

I can still feel you gently holding me, almost cradling me

So, it is like you never left.

A Win

I smile

Every time our eyes meet

As your steps make their way to me

Every time I see you

This was more than what I could have ever hoped for

I am happy that it has finally happened

Like a Fool

What should I do

To show you how much I care about you

To show you much you mean to me

I have all these thoughts buzzing inside my head

Every time your near or far away

I have all these ideas and plans just pilling up like a stack of overdue bills

My hands always long to hold you close

For just a second longer

My body inches closer to fill up any gaps between us

It always makes its way into the warm embrace of your arms

The only place that feels like safety

The only place where time stands still

The world goes quiet

My lips talk nonstop

About everything and nothing all at the same time
My lips form smiles
So many smiles
I wonder if it is possible to ever grow tired of this habit

I feel like a fool every time
I show you how much I care
How much you mean to me

The Next Meet

If we should meet again
By chance or coincidence
Want to know what I will do first

I will not kiss your lips
I will not hold your hands
I will not snuggle up to you
I will stop apologizing so much
You do the same

Every time we meet
We end up apologizing for something
Or the other
 I wonder why that is
I try to be myself
Maybe I am too harsh

On you
On myself

I will forget all my worries
I will not bring up my troubles
I will sit in silence
If that is what you want
I have only a handful of hours
To spend with you after all

Words From the Heart

I think of all the ways I love you
I think of all the reasons why I love you
I wonder if I could pen everything down

Midnight talks
Strolls and stories
I have told you of all the ways others have hurt me
You cared enough to quietly listen
You never once replicated that behavior

Anger
Sadness
Grief
Disappointment
I did not have to hold in these emotions
You were always there to hold my hands instead

Laughter
Inside jokes
Dates and Debates
Shielded me from the worries and annoyances
Of the world

Every Prayer
Every Embrace
Every Kiss
Every Touch
Showed me how loved I was in return

I know I do not say this
Nearly enough,
So, I will put it in writing
I love you dearly
I miss you the most

Livin'

I do not think so much about death
About dying
When I am around you
Is this what healing feels like
Or is just love

Sinner

I have broken the rules

Tore down every boundary I had set for myself

Loving you feels right even it is the wrong thing to do

Might even be sinful

The thought of losing you

Feels like a punishment in this life and the next

I know I am a handful

Practically a hazard

Sharp bloody edges

If there is anything of beauty that resides in me

You saw it first

I still do not see anything

While I continue to doubt myself

Again, and again

My love for you

Is the purest part of me

Opening Up

My lips spilled kisses

My lips spilled secrets

When you listen

When you hold me close

You tear away the pages of my unforgettable past

Messy torn pages yellowed with age

Tear stains

Blood stains

Ink stains

It will not be long till you reach the end

The very last page

Burn the book to ashes

There will finally be room

For new moments and memories

Challenge

I would rather show you that I love you in one hundred different ways

Then tell you that I love you one hundred times over

I fear that one lifetime might not enough to accomplish this

So, I pray that you stay mine in the afterlife too.

Dawn's Eyes

I have seen the moon shrouded in darkness

I have seen the night sky splattered with stars

I have seen clouds and rain looming over my head

I have seen endless snow

Nothing spectacular

But now I see the sun

In your eyes

Bright and beautiful

I am not a morning person at all

But I always hope to always see the sun rise in the morning

Overdoing It

Please do not misunderstand me

Please do not get scared

I tend to overdo things when in love

Over care

Over trust

Over love

Over accept

So, I know I will love you more then you love me

So, I know that I will need you more then you will need me

Perhaps it is due to the pains of the past

Maybe even the lessons I have learnt along the way

Or just simply because I can

The Gift of Love

There was no fancy packaging, bow or card attached

It still found it's way to me

You have given me the gift of love

It was unexpected and unpredictable

It was what I did not know I needed at the time

It was more then I deserved

A love that is pure

A love free from serious heartache

A love that makes me smile

A love that made me cherish every single moment that was spent with you

It made time fly by

It made me want to snatch away the hands of the clock every time we met

Stretch out single moments that only lasted a second

This gift of love was colorful and beautiful in its own unpredictable way

Melted Promises

You made love feel simple and safe

It was a gift that was so easy to accept and give back in return

Dreams

It does not take money to dream they say

I suppose it is all right to relive them from time to time

The dreams where it is just you and I

Everything looks perfect

Feels perfect

Where the colors are bright and never dull

Where the sounds are crisp and never flat

Where the people walk around with rosy cheeks and twinkling eyes

Have a bounce in their steps

We hold hands

I smile in every single one of them

Time passes on quick

The sky never darkens

You talk of the happy days ahead

I continue to walk down the path

Without a care in the world

Until one day I dreamt of something else

Fear gripped at my heart

I still walked ahead without looking back

The sky was still the same

I could feel my lips hurting from the smile that was plastered on my face

I hoped for your sake it stayed for a second longer

My legs felt weak, and I did not have the energy to move ahead

I feared that heartbreak is just around the corner

I did not know how to save you from it either

Home

Support

Comfort

Shelter

Happiness

Joy

You have been all that and more

Much like one's home

One that welcomed me in with ease and comfort

Never had to worry about overstaying my welcome

Never had to care about repairs and appearances

I finally felt what could only be described as happiness

Acceptance

Unfortunately, now I feel that I am far away from happiness, comfort, and safety

It is only a matter of time before I will be forced to pack up

Never look back

Leave behind the key

Unpack and start all over again

I really wanted to stay longer

Double Ended Sword

Love has been described as many things as possible over time

For me it looks and feels like a double ended sword

Long thin and razor sharp

Hurts the most in the daytime

It gleams in the dark

One side is wedged inside me

The other in you

If I come closer to you it goes in deeper

If I pull away it will hurt you

You will be the one bleeding

I do not want that

I do not know how to pull away either

Fading

I know now that time will not heal everything for me
Though I hope it does for you
Hearts are fragile
Fragile things break
No matter how careful we are with them
Never on purpose
Always by accident
So, things are moving along
Just like they should
I do not want you to go
I cannot even make you stay
I do not want you to be a mere string of memories
I do not want you to be just a handful of pictures
I do not want you to be countless messages and texts
I do not want you to be the pages to a conversation
I will hold on to everything anyway

Betraying every word that makes up this poem

Even then

I still do not want you to go away

Final Message

This is not the end

Only the beginning to something else

This is not goodbye

Just trying to find a different place for you in my heart

About the Author

Farzana Habib

Farzana Habib is a 31 and a full time Scorpio who resides in Laval Quebec. She is a certified daycare educator and a student studying English and Education at Concordia University. She wants to work as a teacher and counselor after graduation. When she is away from her writing desk and computer, she can be found outside sightseeing volunteering or simply meeting new people and learning about different cultures.

www.ingramcontent.com/pod-product-compliance
Lightning Source LLC
LaVergne TN
LVHW041600070526
838199LV00046B/2066